VADER DOWN: VOLUME 5

It is a period of unrest. Darth Vader has tracked his son, the rebel pilot Luke Skywalker, to the planet Vrogas Vas. The pair crash-landed, only to be stranded planetside and faced with new enemies.

Han Solo, Chewbacca, and R2-D2 successfully rescued Luke from Dr. Aphra and her droids, 0-0-0 and BT-1, but had little time to retreat before the Wookiee Black Krrsantan intervened.

Elsewhere, Princess Leia's search for Darth Vader brought her face-to-face with the Sith Lord. Ordering all surviving rebel pilots to attack with full force, she called for a strike that could end her as quickly as it could Vader.

As the rebels rush in, Luke rushed to rescue the Princess from certain death. Meanwhile, Commander Karbin has arrived, changing the fate of this rebel attack....

JASON AARON	MIKE DEODATO	FRANK MARTIN JR.	CHRIS ELIOPOULOS
Writer	Artist	Colorist	Letterer
MARK BROOKS	HEATHER ANTOS	JORDAN D. WHITE	Story By JASON AARON & KIERON GILLEN
Cover Artist	Assistant Editor	Editor	
C.B. CEBULSKI	AXEL ALONSO	JOE QUESADA	DAN BUCKLEY
Executive Editor	Editor In Chief	Chief Creative Officer	Publisher

For Lucasfilm:
Senior Editor FRANK PARISI
Creative Director MICHAEL SIGLAIN
Lucasfilm Story Group RAYNE ROBERTS, PABLO HIDALGO, LELAND CHEE

ABDO
Spotlight

ABDOPUBLISHING.COM

Reinforced library bound edition published in 2017 by Spotlight,
a division of ABDO, PO Box 398166, Minneapolis, Minnesota 55439.
Spotlight produces high-quality reinforced library bound editions for
schools and libraries. Published by agreement with Marvel Characters, Inc.

Printed in the United States of America, North Mankato, Minnesota.
092016
012017

 THIS BOOK CONTAINS
RECYCLED MATERIALS

PUBLISHER'S CATALOGING IN PUBLICATION DATA

Names: Aaron, Jason ; Gillen, Kieron authors. | Deodato, Mike ; Martin, Laura ;
   Larroca, Salvador ; Delgado, Edgar, illustrators.
Title: Vader Down / writers: Jason Aaron ; Kieron Gillen ; art: Mike Deodato;
   Laura Martin ; Salvador Larroca ; Edgar Delgado.
Description: Reinforced library bound edition. | Minneapolis, Minnesota : Spotlight,
   2017. | Series: Star Wars : Vader Down
Summary: Darth Vader tracks Luke Skywalker's location to Vrogas Vas, but when
   they're stranded on the planet, they face new enemies and challenges.
Identifiers: LCCN 2016941801 | ISBN 9781614795612 (volume 1) | ISBN
   9781614795629 (volume 2) | ISBN 9781614795636 (volume 3) | ISBN
   9781614795643 (volume 4) | ISBN 9781614795650 (volume 5) | ISBN
   9781614795667 (volume 6)
Subjects: LCSH: Vader, Darth (Fictitious character)--Juvenile fiction. | Star Wars
   fiction--Comic books, strips, etc.--Juvenile fiction. | Graphic novels--Juvenile
   fiction.
Classification: DDC 741.5--dc23
LC record available at https://lccn.loc.gov/2016941801

Spotlight

A Division of ABDO
abdopublishing.com

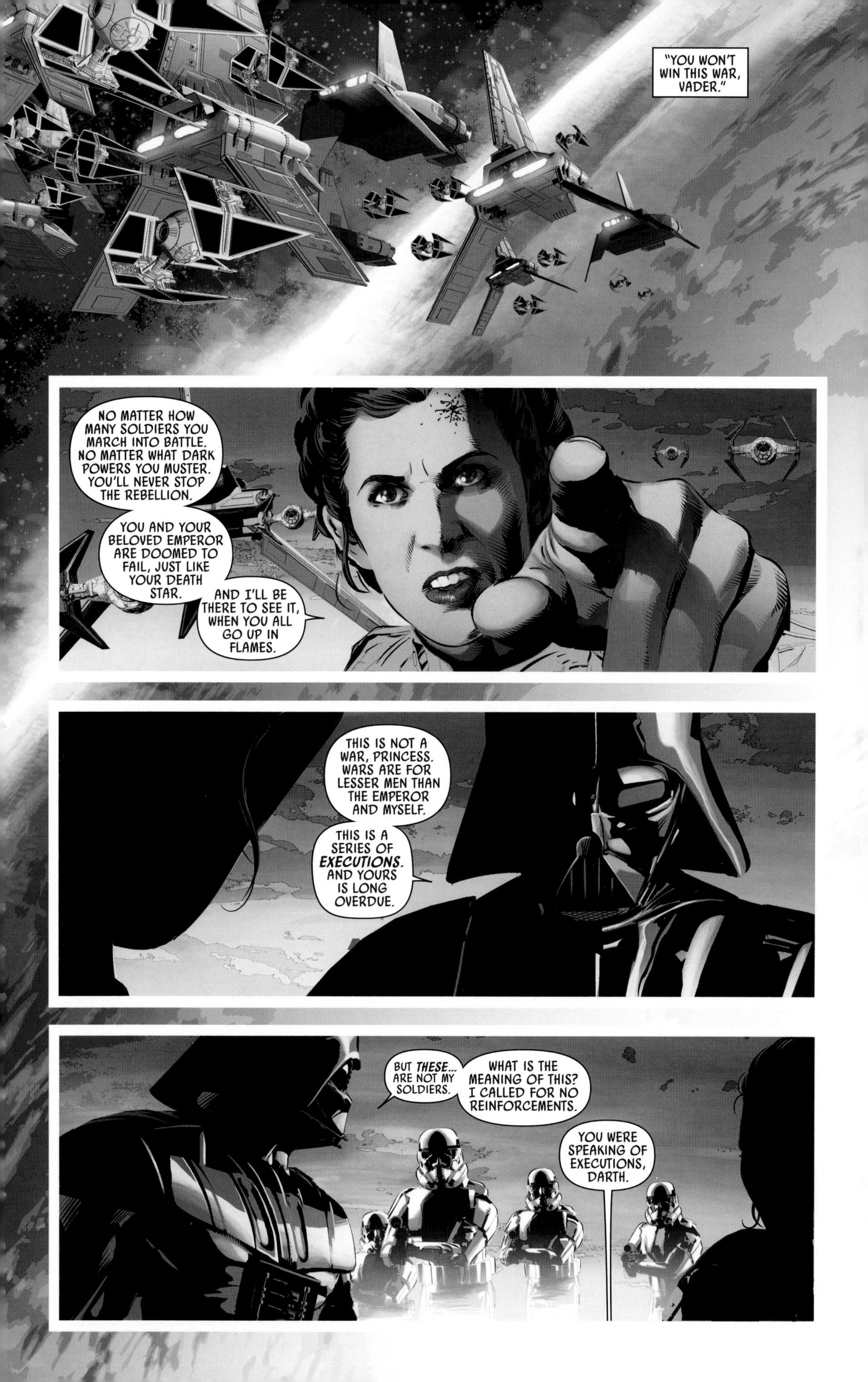

"YOU WON'T WIN THIS WAR, VADER."
NO MATTER HOW MANY SOLDIERS YOU MARCH INTO BATTLE. NO MATTER WHAT DARK POWERS YOU MUSTER. YOU'LL NEVER STOP THE REBELLION.
YOU AND YOUR BELOVED EMPEROR ARE DOOMED TO FAIL, JUST LIKE YOUR DEATH STAR.
AND I'LL BE THERE TO SEE IT, WHEN YOU ALL GO UP IN FLAMES.
THIS IS NOT A WAR, PRINCESS. WARS ARE FOR LESSER MEN THAN THE EMPEROR AND MYSELF.
THIS IS A SERIES OF EXECUTIONS. AND YOURS IS LONG OVERDUE.
BUT THESE... ARE NOT MY SOLDIERS.
WHAT IS THE MEANING OF THIS? I CALLED FOR NO REINFORCEMENTS.
YOU WERE SPEAKING OF EXECUTIONS, DARTH.

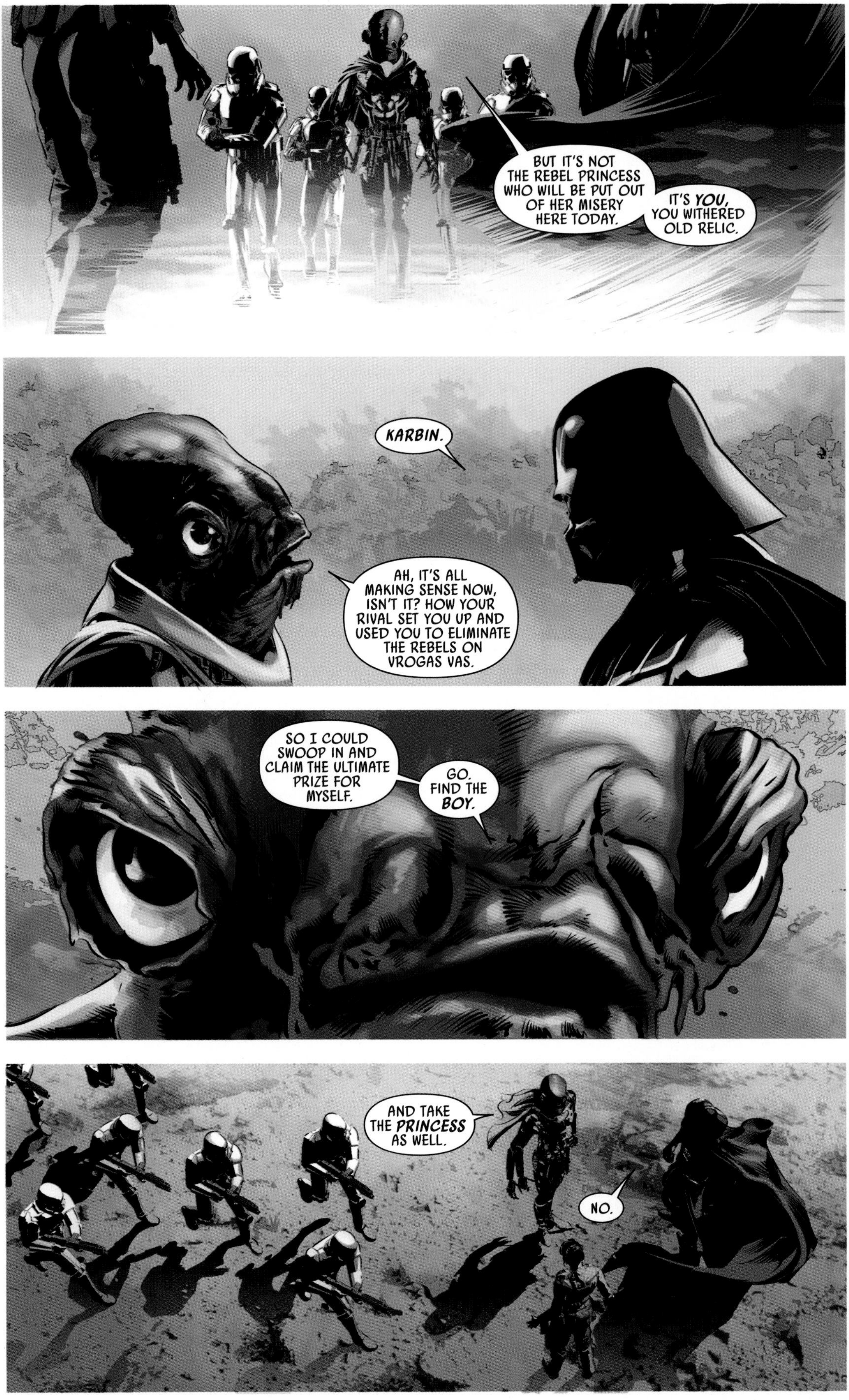
BUT IT'S NOT THE REBEL PRINCESS WHO WILL BE PUT OUT OF HER MISERY HERE TODAY.
IT'S *YOU*, YOU WITHERED OLD RELIC.
KARBIN.
AH, IT'S ALL MAKING SENSE NOW, ISN'T IT? HOW YOUR RIVAL SET YOU UP AND USED YOU TO ELIMINATE THE REBELS ON VROGAS VAS.
SO I COULD SWOOP IN AND CLAIM THE ULTIMATE PRIZE FOR MYSELF.
GO. FIND THE *BOY.*
AND TAKE THE *PRINCESS* AS WELL.
NO.

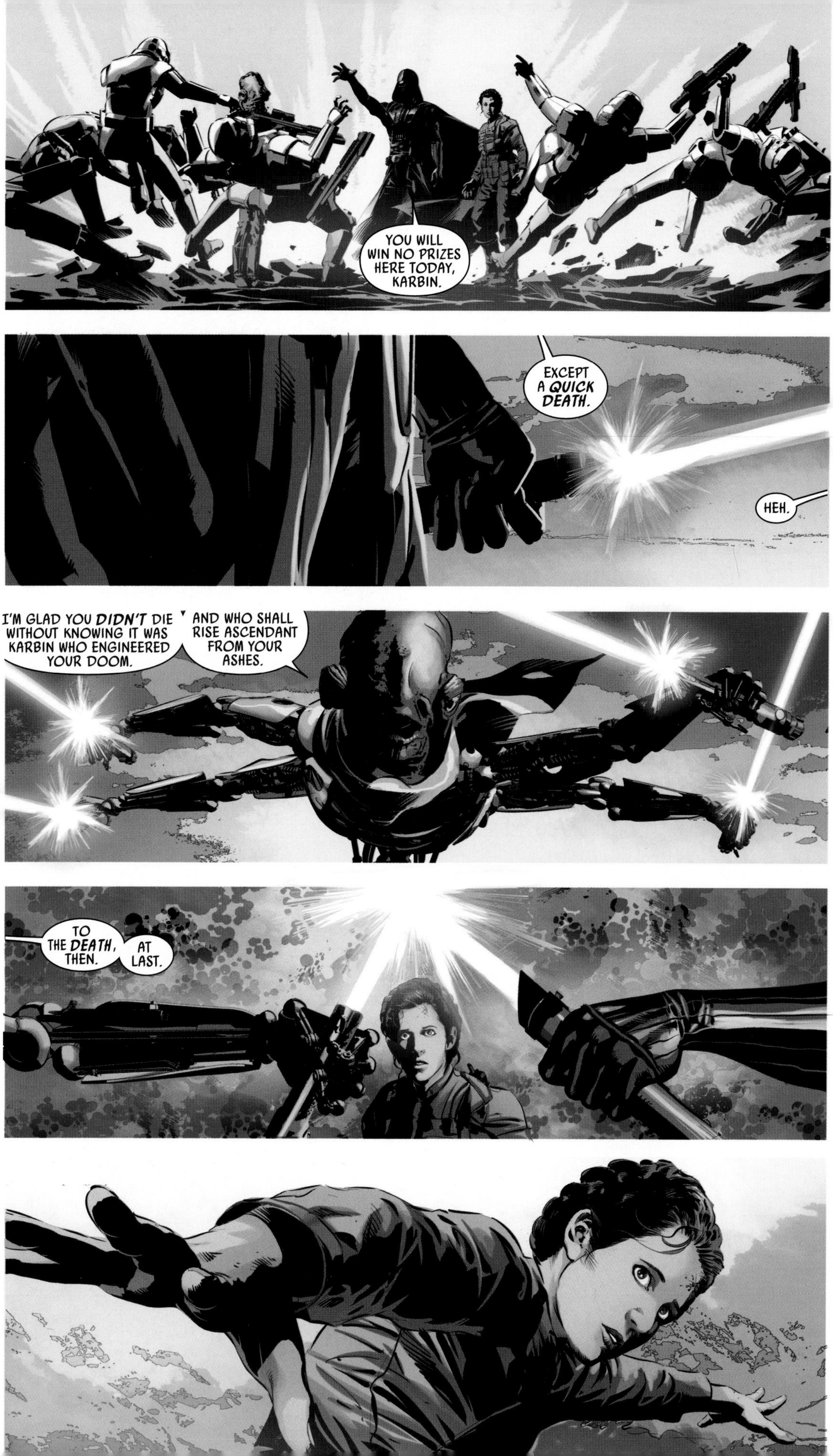
YOU WILL WIN NO PRIZES HERE TODAY, KARBIN.
EXCEPT A QUICK DEATH.
HEH.
I'M GLAD YOU DIDN'T DIE WITHOUT KNOWING IT WAS KARBIN WHO ENGINEERED YOUR DOOM.
AND WHO SHALL RISE ASCENDANT FROM YOUR ASHES.
TO THE DEATH, THEN.
AT LAST.

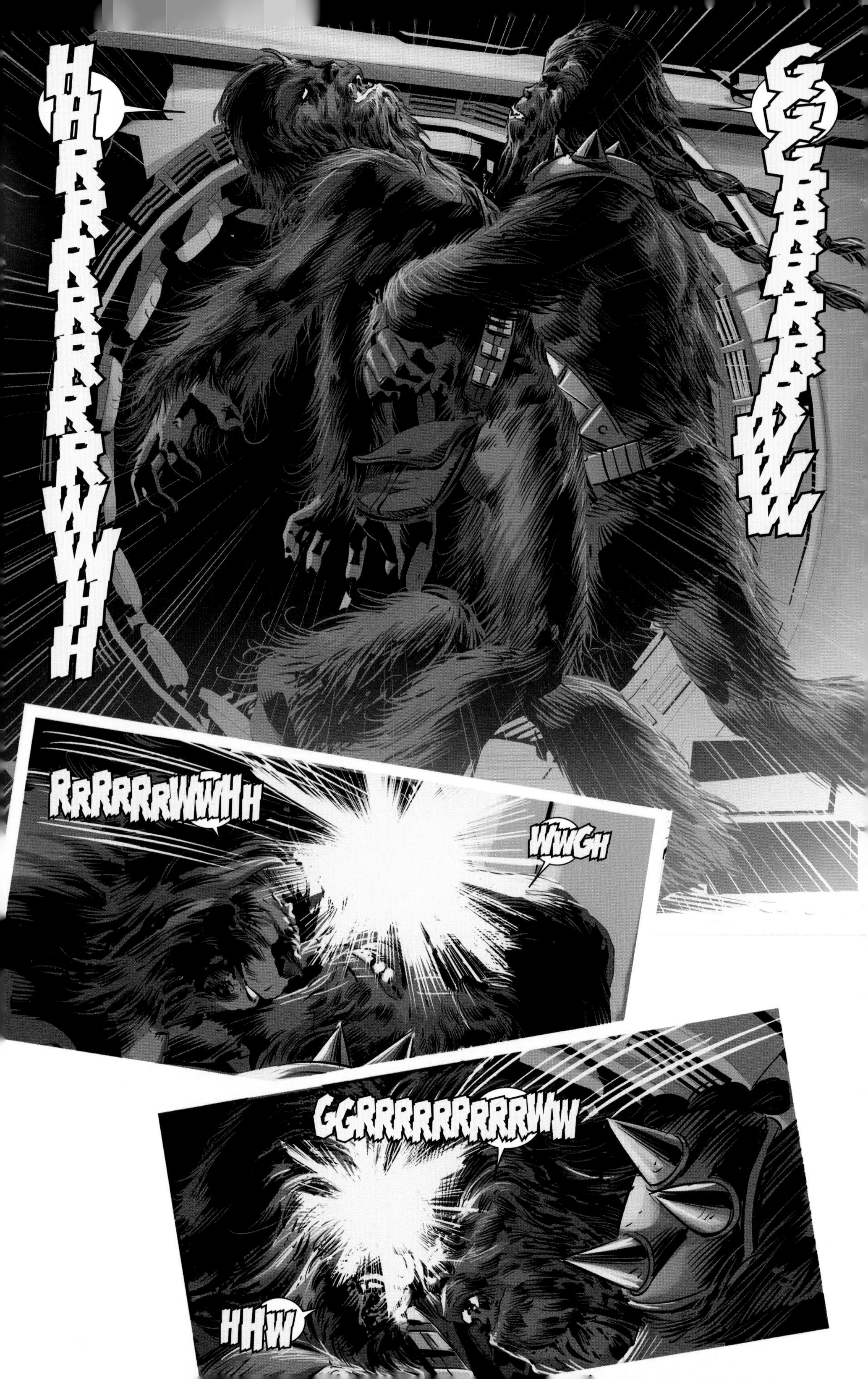
HHRRRRRRRRWWHH
GGGRRRRRRWW
RRRRRRWWHH
WWGH
GGRRRRRRRRRRWW
HHW

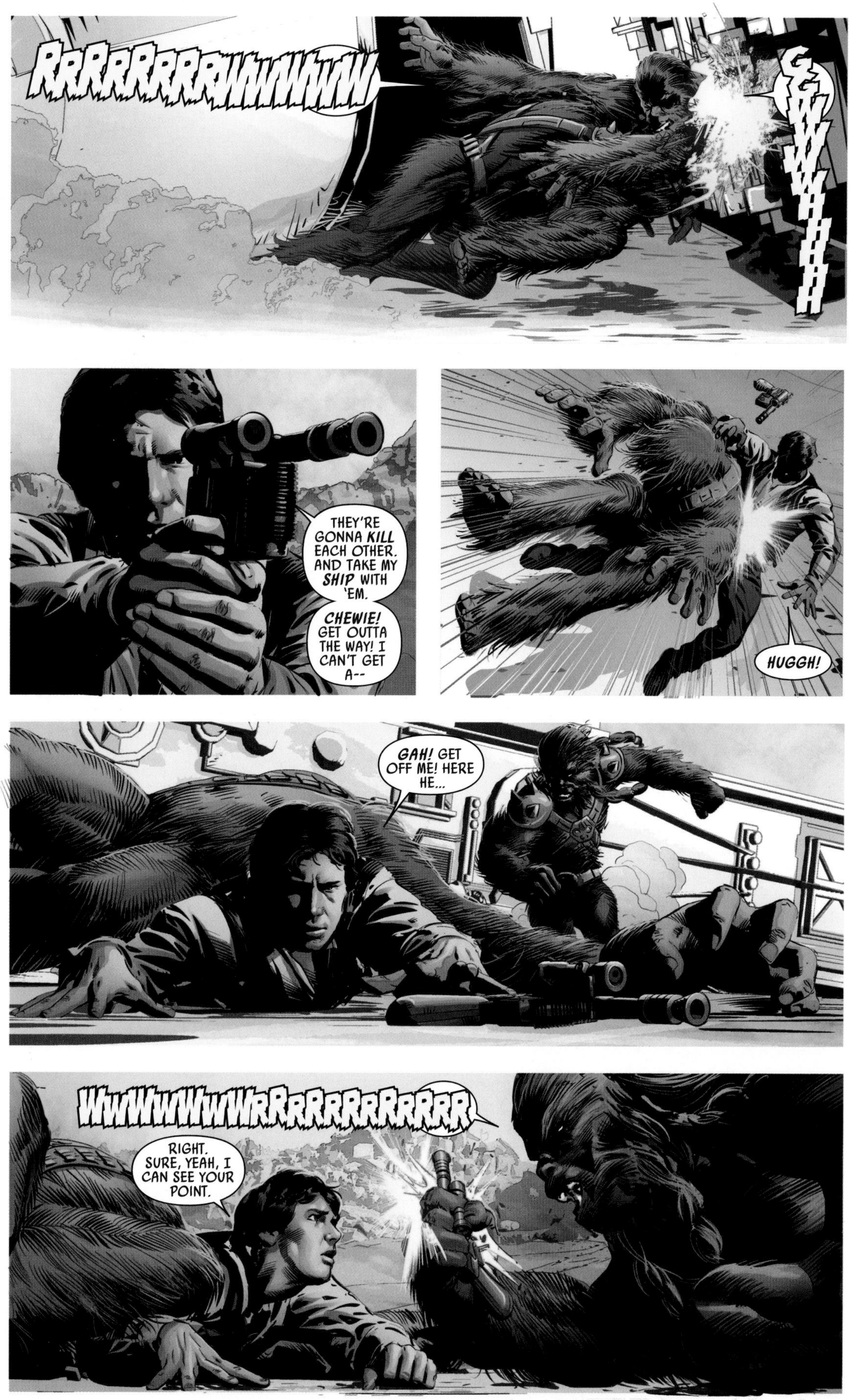

RRRRRRRRWWWWWW
GGWWWHHHH
THEY'RE GONNA KILL EACH OTHER. AND TAKE MY SHIP WITH 'EM.
CHEWIE! GET OUTTA THE WAY! I CAN'T GET A--
HUGGH!
GAH! GET OFF ME! HERE HE...
WWWWWWWWRRRRRRRRRRR
RIGHT. SURE, YEAH, I CAN SEE YOUR POINT.

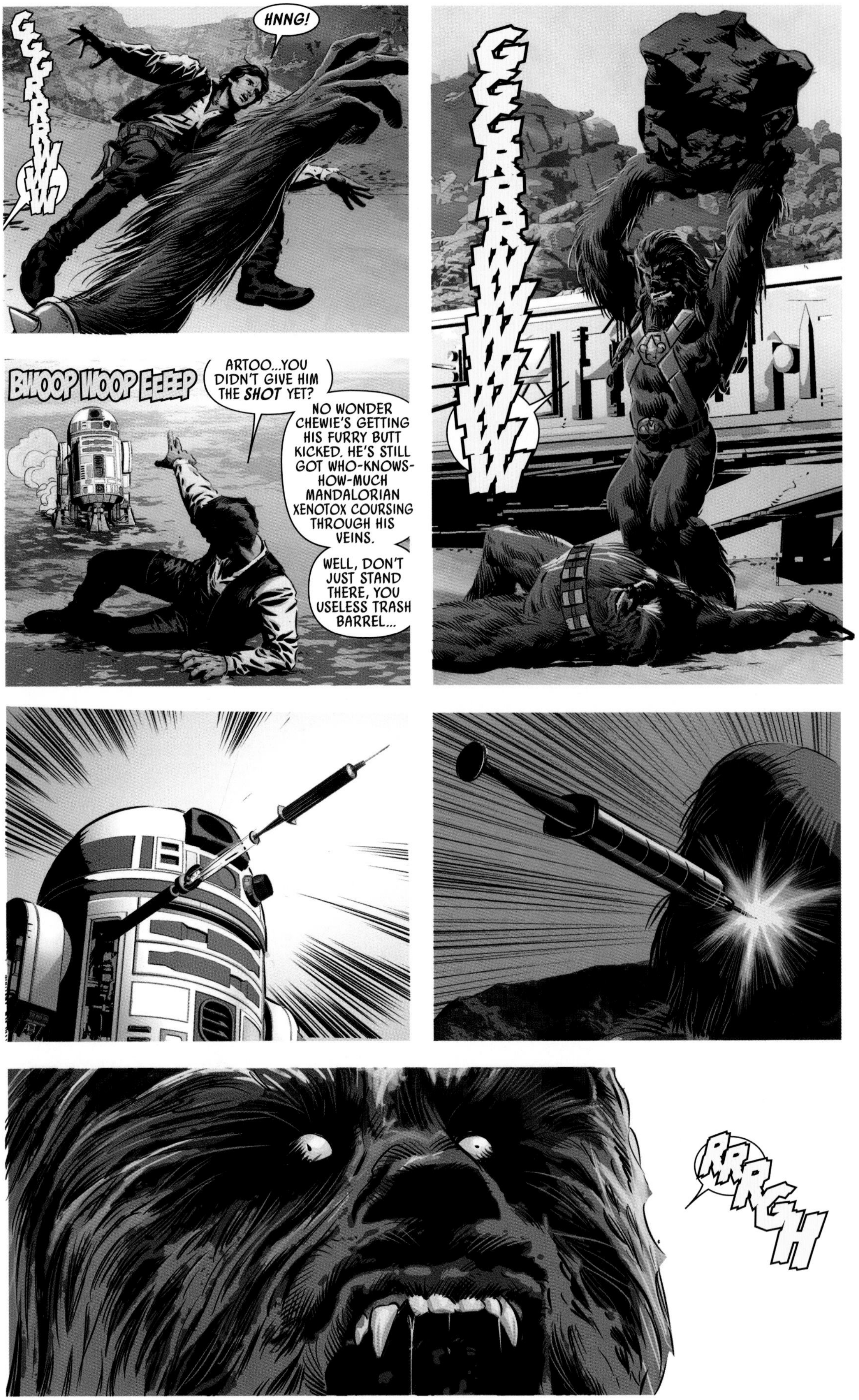
GGGRRRWWW
HNNG!
GGGRRRWWWWWWW
BWOOP WOOP EEEEP
ARTOO...YOU DIDN'T GIVE HIM THE SHOT YET?
NO WONDER CHEWIE'S GETTING HIS FURRY BUTT KICKED. HE'S STILL GOT WHO-KNOWS-HOW-MUCH MANDALORIAN XENOTOX COURSING THROUGH HIS VEINS.
WELL, DON'T JUST STAND THERE, YOU USELESS TRASH BARREL...
RRRGH

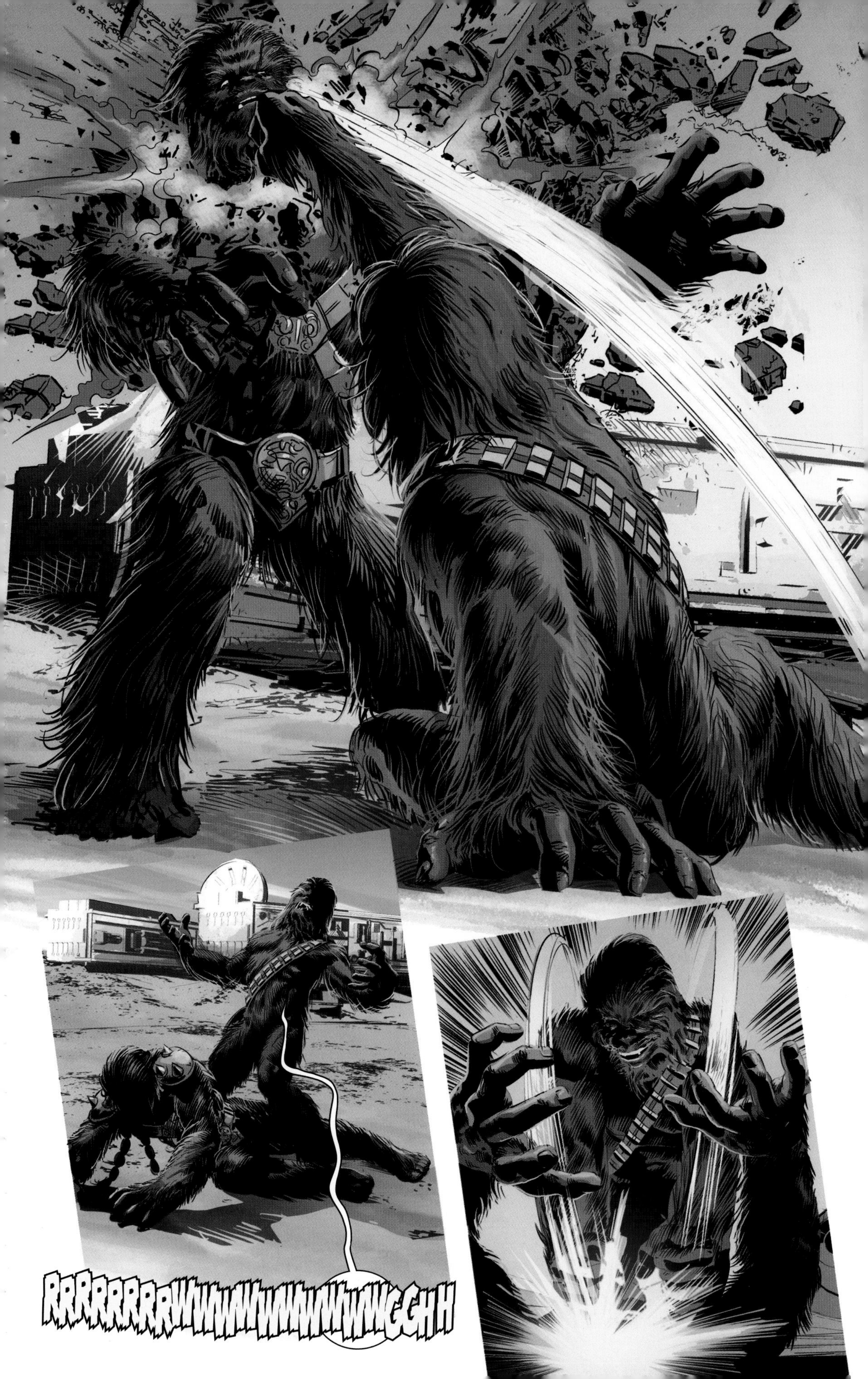
RRRRRRRWWWWWWWWWWWWGGHH

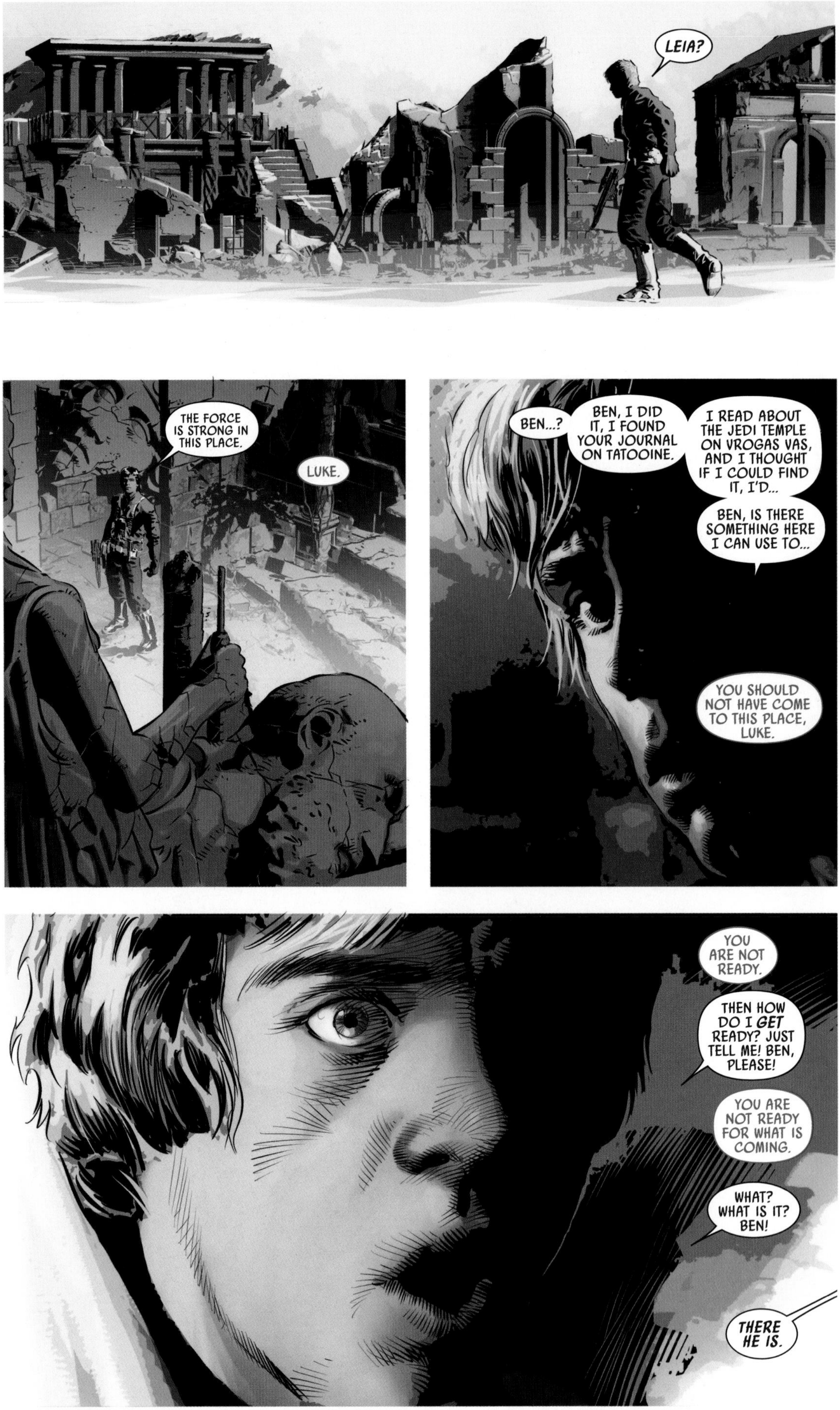
LEIA?
THE FORCE IS STRONG IN THIS PLACE.
LUKE.
BEN...?
BEN, I DID IT, I FOUND YOUR JOURNAL ON TATOOINE.
I READ ABOUT THE JEDI TEMPLE ON VROGAS VAS, AND I THOUGHT IF I COULD FIND IT, I'D...
BEN, IS THERE SOMETHING HERE I CAN USE TO...
YOU SHOULD NOT HAVE COME TO THIS PLACE, LUKE.
YOU ARE NOT READY.
THEN HOW DO I GET READY? JUST TELL ME! BEN, PLEASE!
YOU ARE NOT READY FOR WHAT IS COMING.
WHAT? WHAT IS IT? BEN!
THERE HE IS.

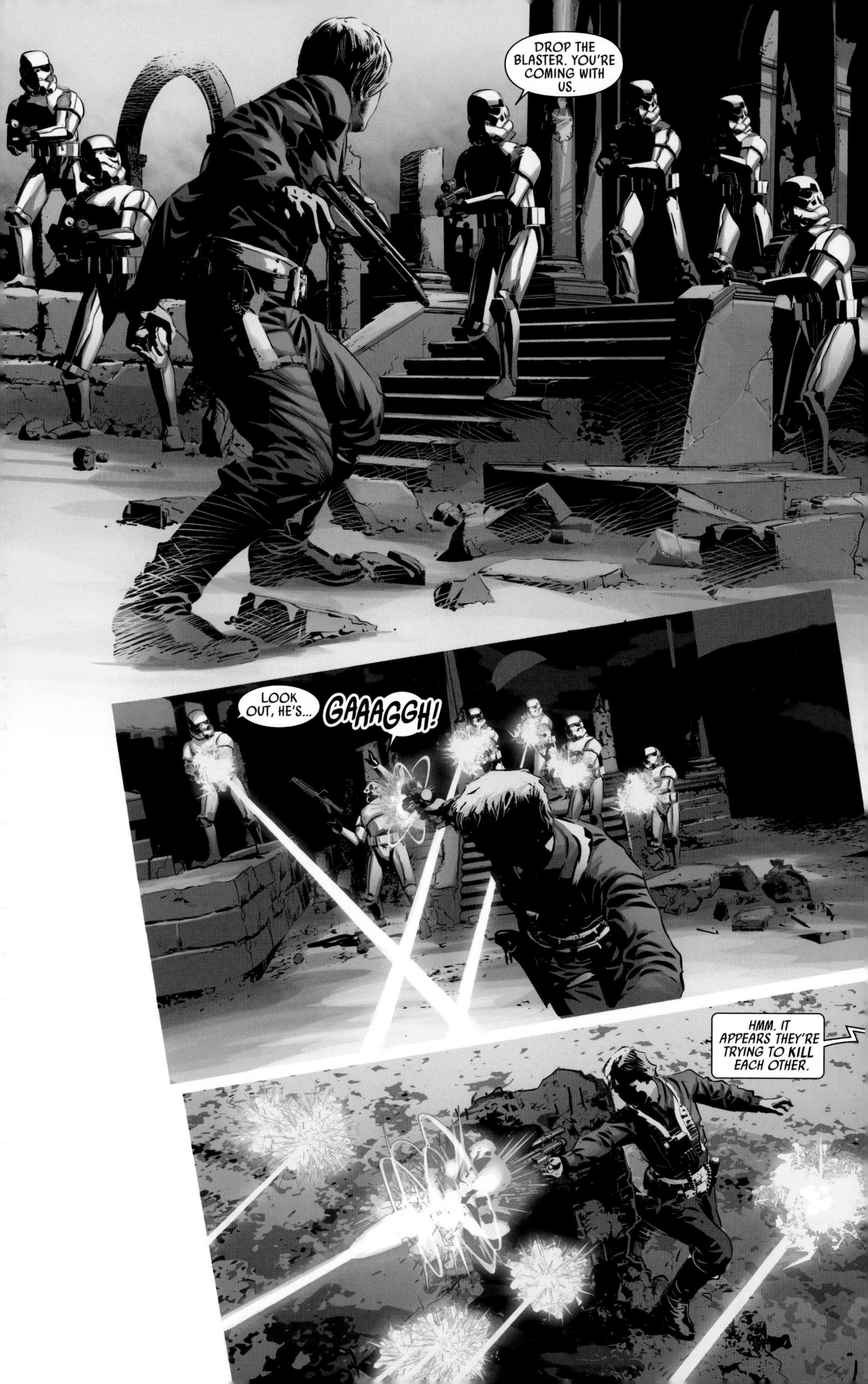
DROP THE BLASTER. YOU'RE COMING WITH US.
LOOK OUT, HE'S...
GAAAGGH!
HMM. IT APPEARS THEY'RE TRYING TO KILL EACH OTHER.

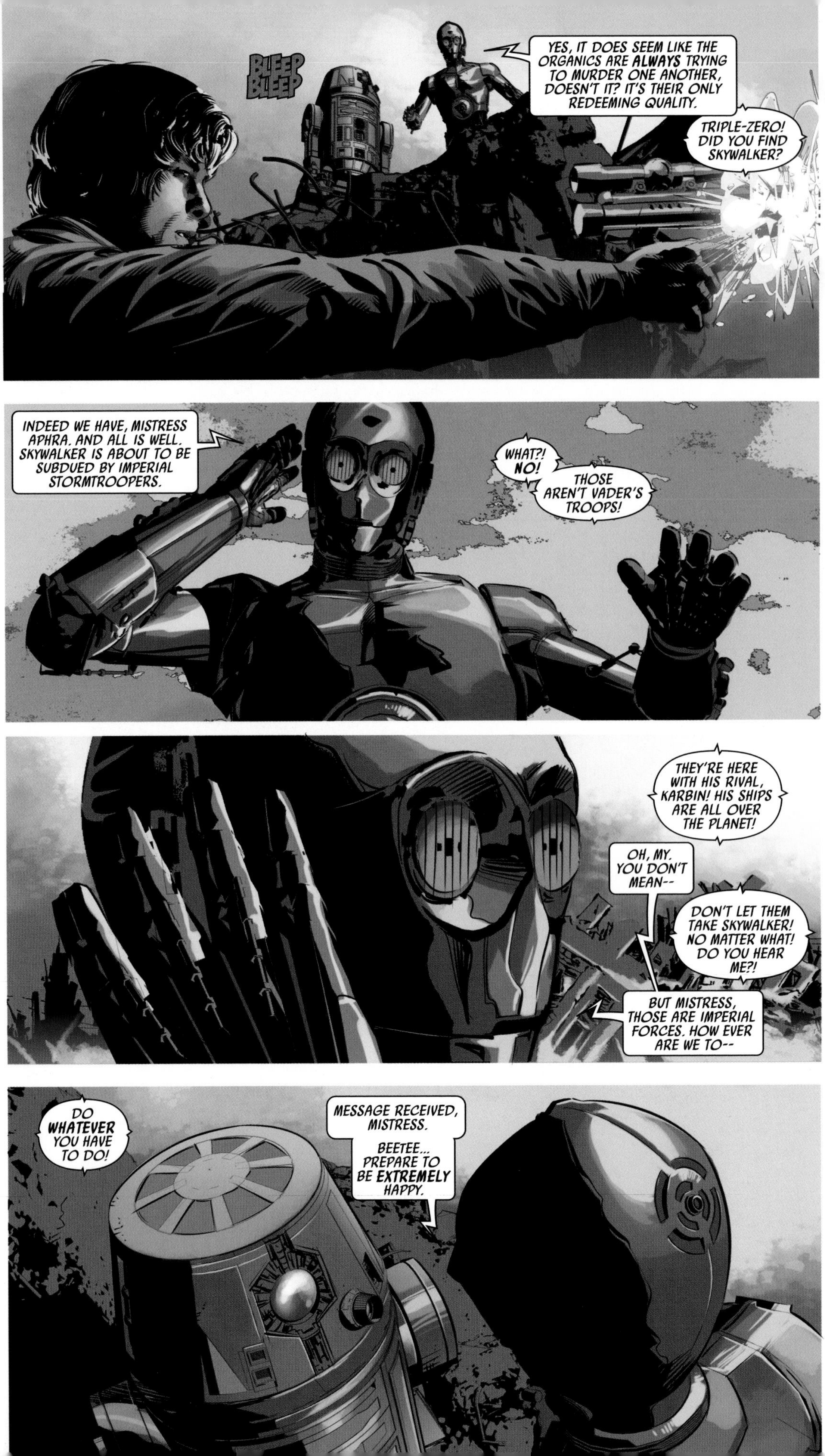
BLEEP BLEEP
YES, IT DOES SEEM LIKE THE ORGANICS ARE ALWAYS TRYING TO MURDER ONE ANOTHER, DOESN'T IT? IT'S THEIR ONLY REDEEMING QUALITY.
TRIPLE-ZERO! DID YOU FIND SKYWALKER?
INDEED WE HAVE, MISTRESS APHRA. AND ALL IS WELL. SKYWALKER IS ABOUT TO BE SUBDUED BY IMPERIAL STORMTROOPERS.
WHAT?! NO!
THOSE AREN'T VADER'S TROOPS!
THEY'RE HERE WITH HIS RIVAL, KARBIN! HIS SHIPS ARE ALL OVER THE PLANET!
OH, MY. YOU DON'T MEAN--
DON'T LET THEM TAKE SKYWALKER! NO MATTER WHAT! DO YOU HEAR ME?!
BUT MISTRESS, THOSE ARE IMPERIAL FORCES. HOW EVER ARE WE TO--
DO WHATEVER YOU HAVE TO DO!
MESSAGE RECEIVED, MISTRESS.
BEETEE... PREPARE TO BE EXTREMELY HAPPY.

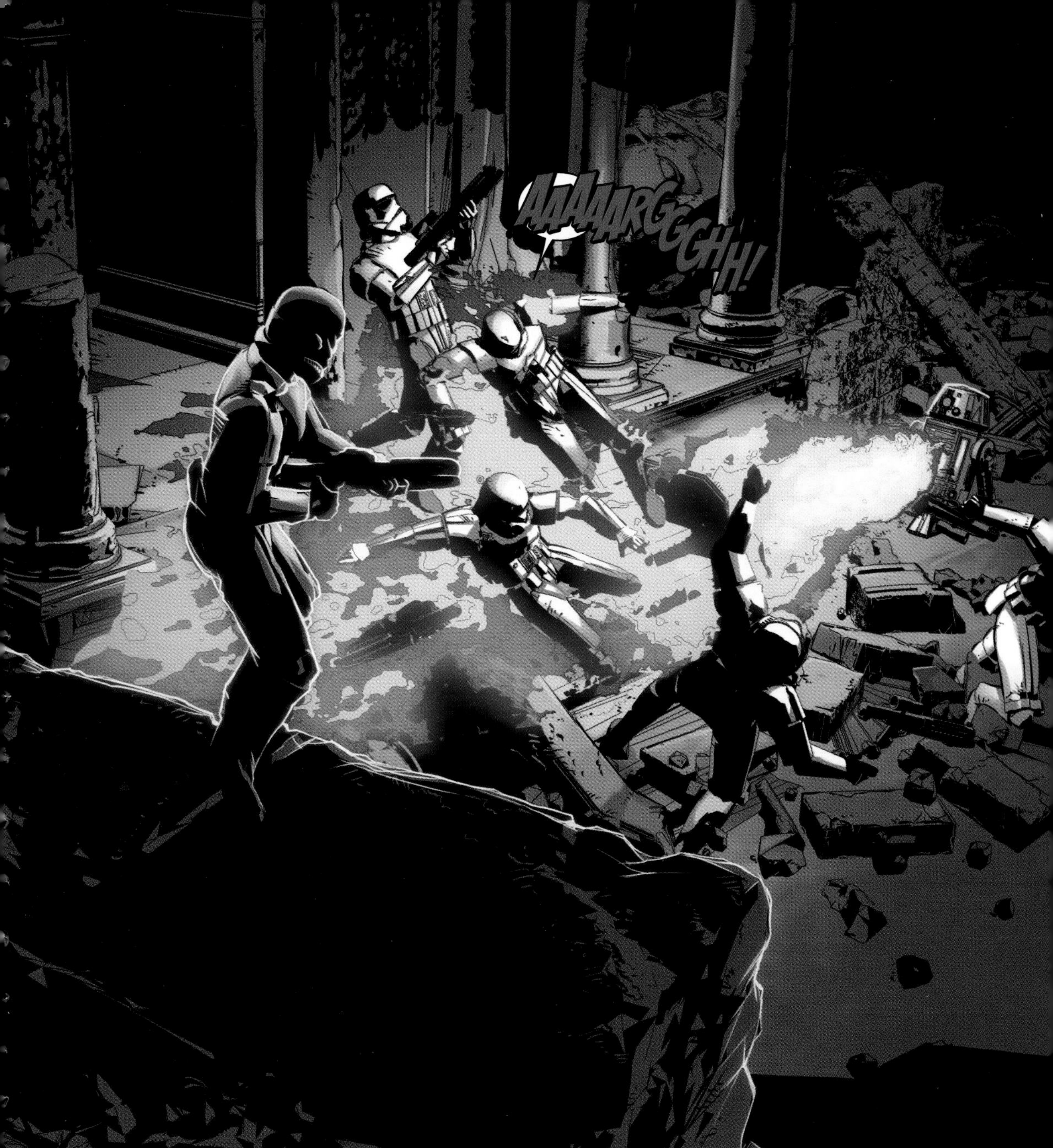
AAAAARGGGHH!

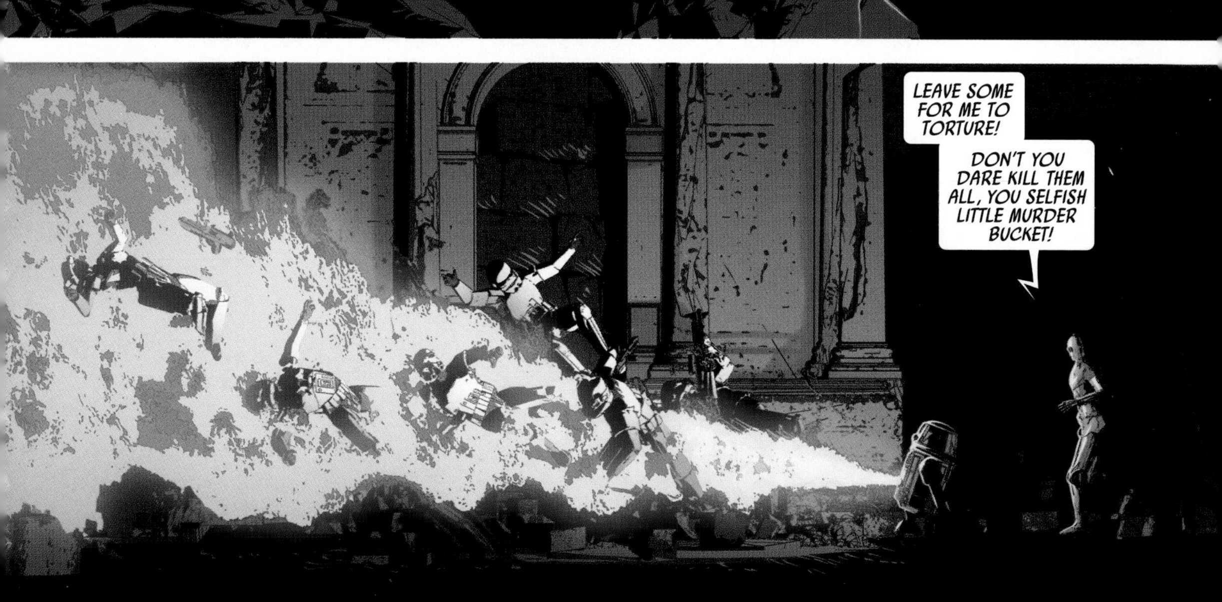
LEAVE SOME FOR ME TO TORTURE!
DON'T YOU DARE KILL THEM ALL, YOU SELFISH LITTLE MURDER BUCKET!

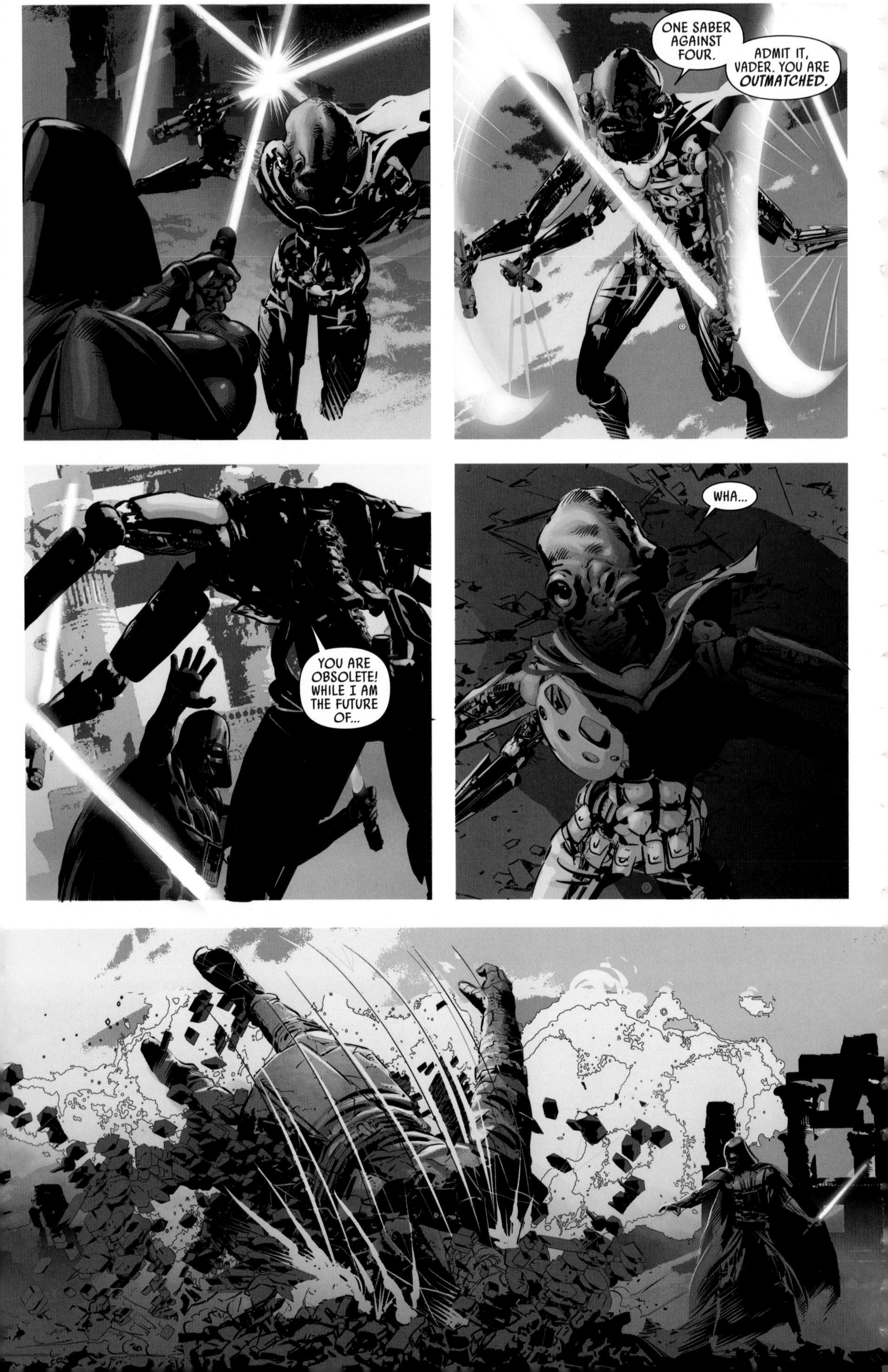
ONE SABER AGAINST FOUR.
ADMIT IT, VADER. YOU ARE OUTMATCHED.
YOU ARE OBSOLETE! WHILE I AM THE FUTURE OF...
WHA...

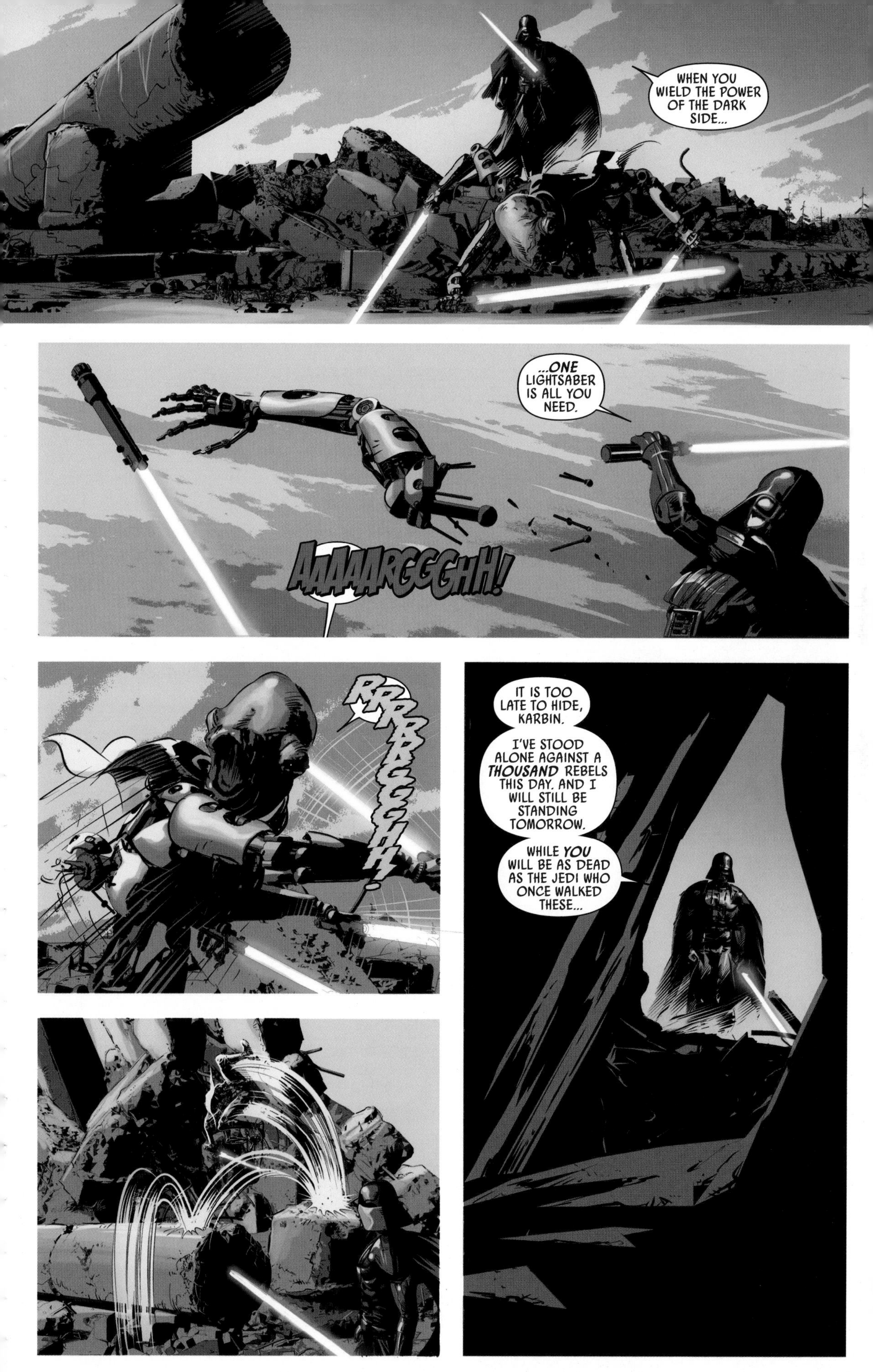
WHEN YOU WIELD THE POWER OF THE DARK SIDE...
...ONE LIGHTSABER IS ALL YOU NEED.
AAAAARGGGHH!
RRRRRGGGHH!
IT IS TOO LATE TO HIDE, KARBIN.
I'VE STOOD ALONE AGAINST A THOUSAND REBELS THIS DAY. AND I WILL STILL BE STANDING TOMORROW.
WHILE YOU WILL BE AS DEAD AS THE JEDI WHO ONCE WALKED THESE...

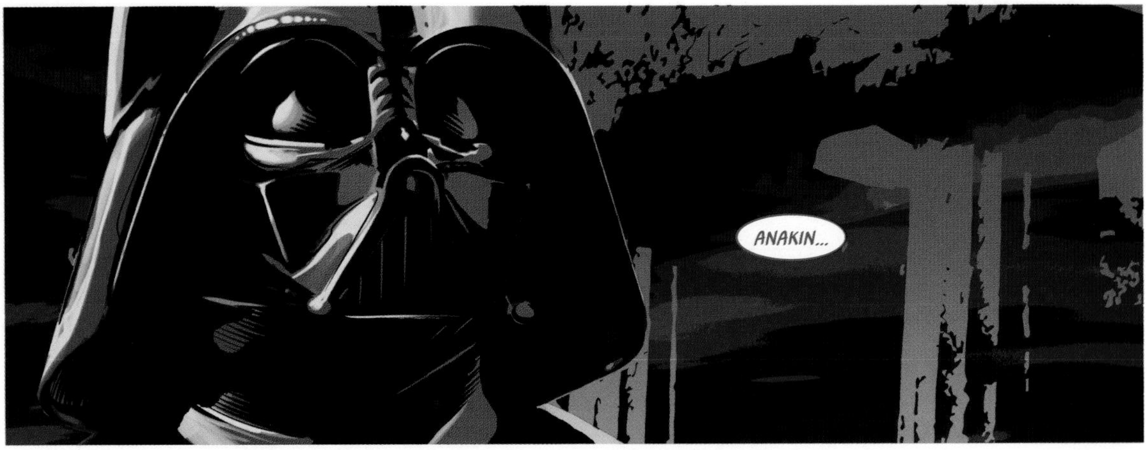
ANAKIN...

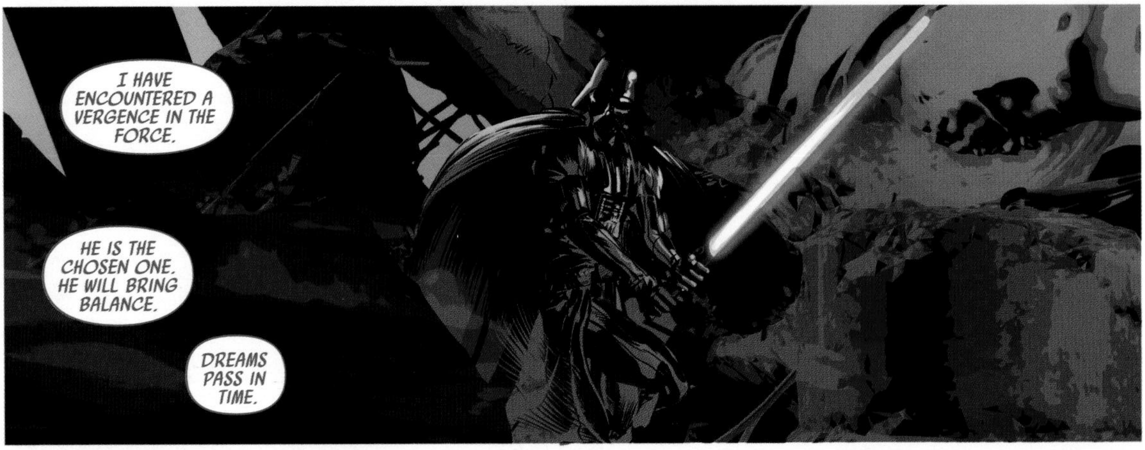
I HAVE ENCOUNTERED A VERGENCE IN THE FORCE.
HE IS THE CHOSEN ONE. HE WILL BRING BALANCE.
DREAMS PASS IN TIME.

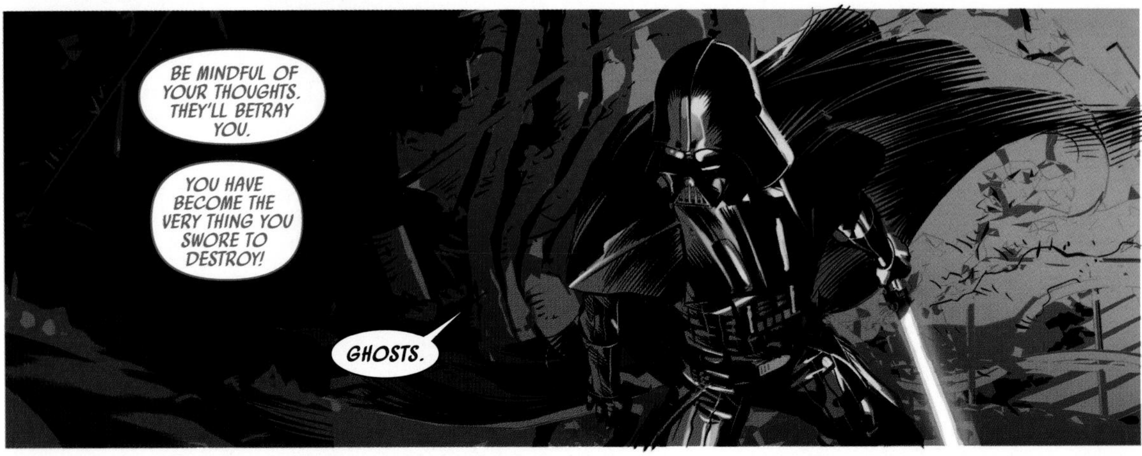
BE MINDFUL OF YOUR THOUGHTS. THEY'LL BETRAY YOU.
YOU HAVE BECOME THE VERY THING YOU SWORE TO DESTROY!
GHOSTS.

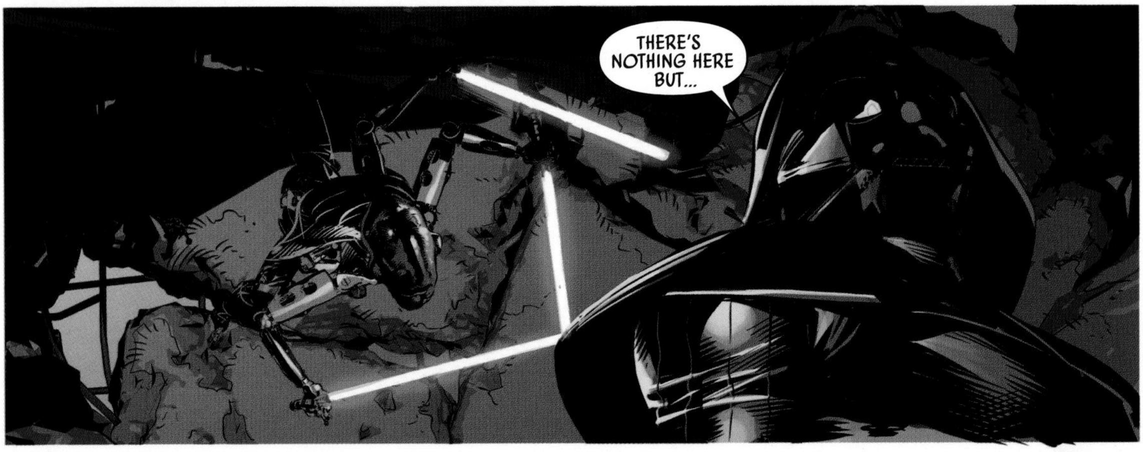
THERE'S NOTHING HERE BUT...

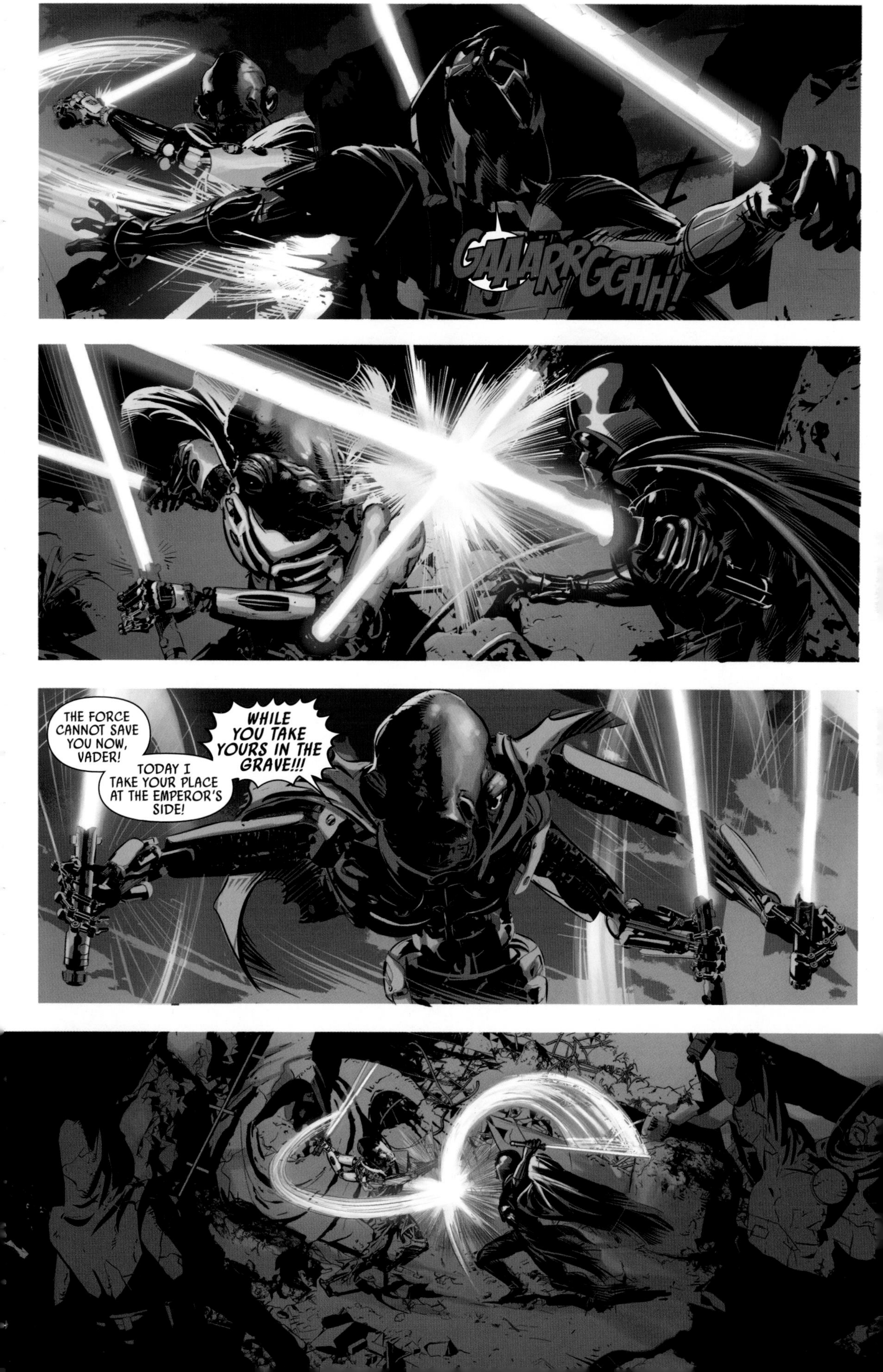
GAAARRGGHH!
THE FORCE CANNOT SAVE YOU NOW, VADER!
TODAY I TAKE YOUR PLACE AT THE EMPEROR'S SIDE!
WHILE YOU TAKE YOURS IN THE GRAVE!!!

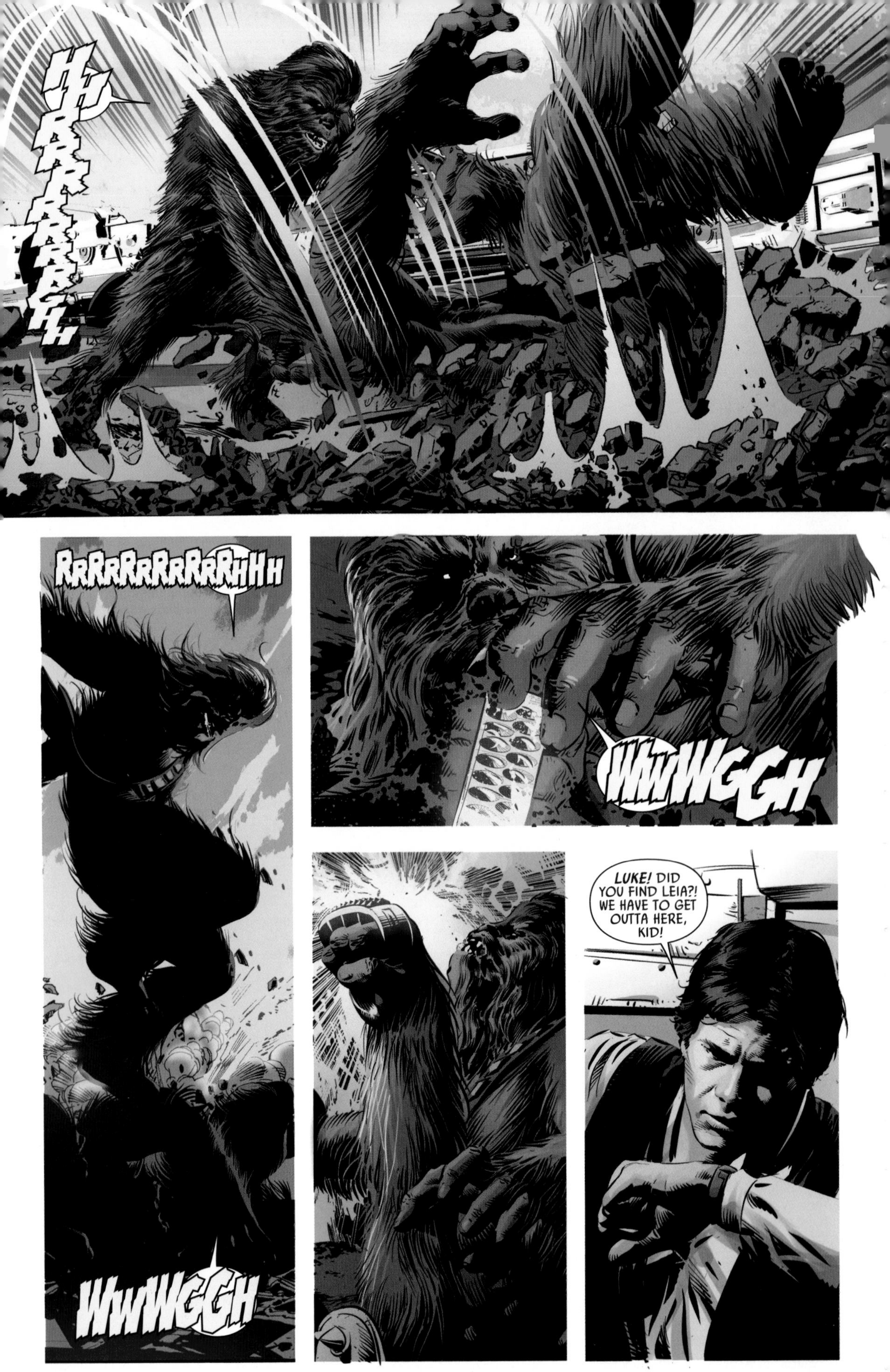
HHRRRRRRRGHH
RRRRRRRRRRRRHHH
WWWGGH
WWWGGH
LUKE! DID YOU FIND LEIA?! WE HAVE TO GET OUTTA HERE, KID!

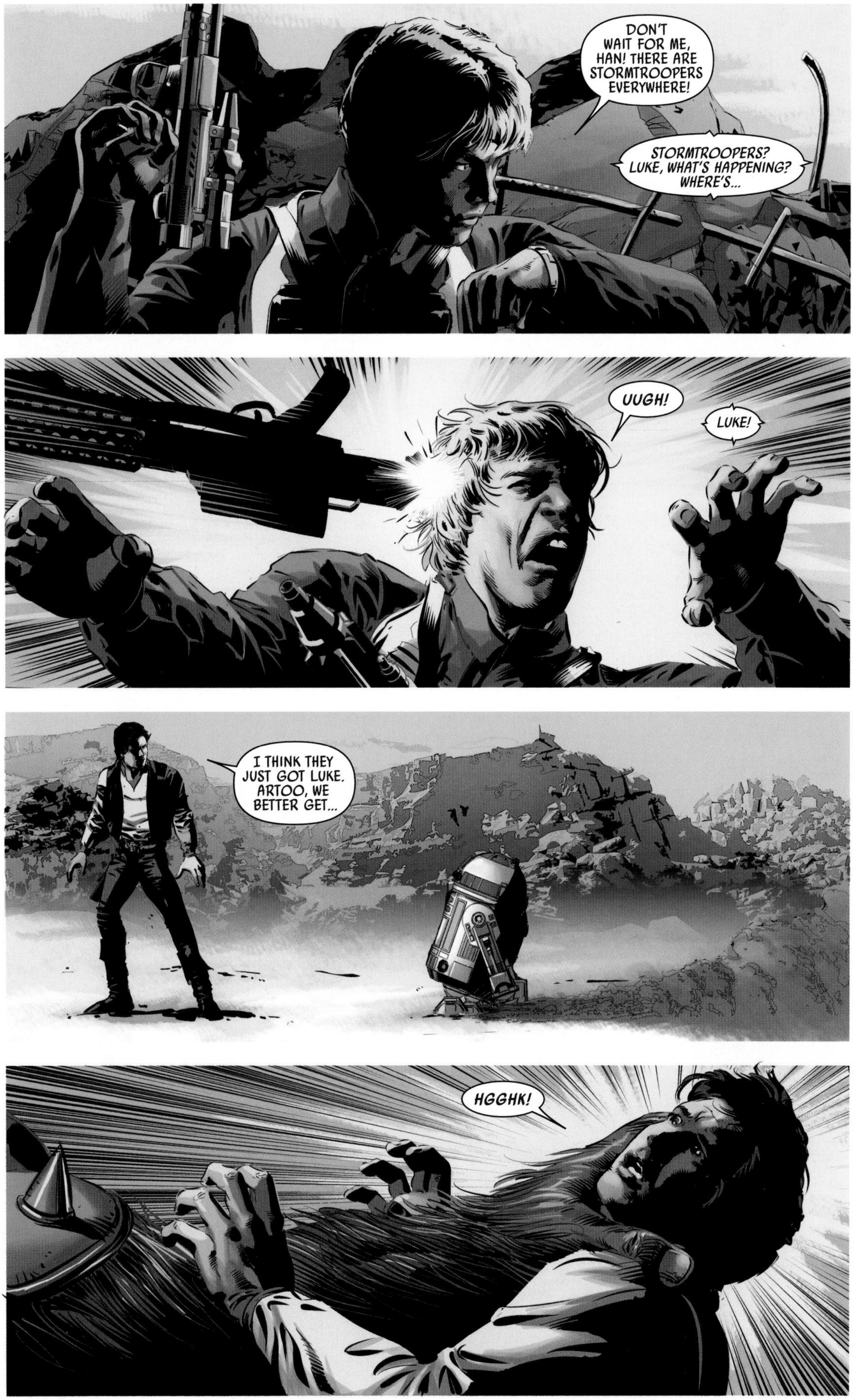
DON'T WAIT FOR ME, HAN! THERE ARE STORMTROOPERS EVERYWHERE!
STORMTROOPERS? LUKE, WHAT'S HAPPENING? WHERE'S...
UUGH!
LUKE!
I THINK THEY JUST GOT LUKE. ARTOO, WE BETTER GET...
HGGHK!

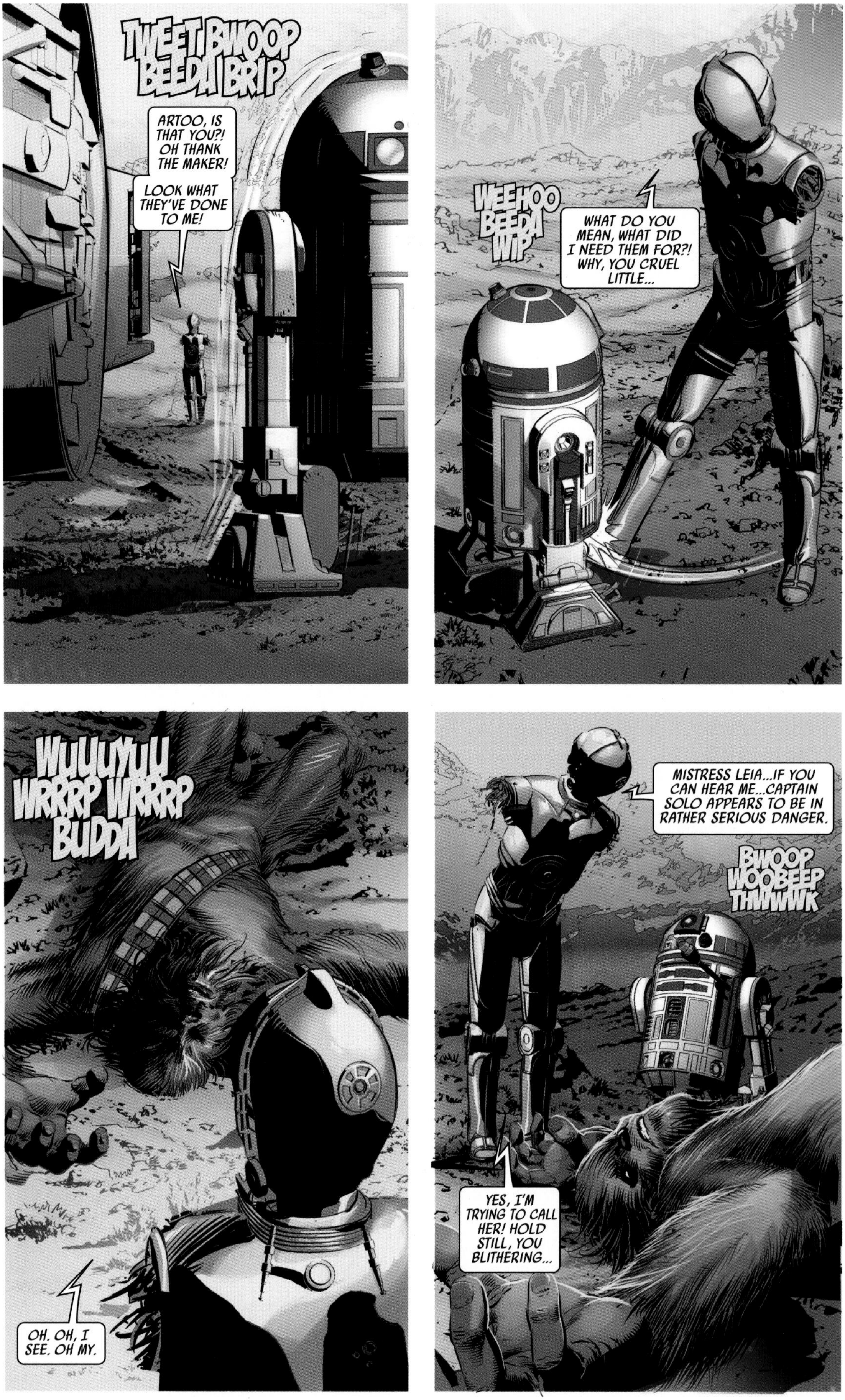
TWEET BWOOP BEEDA BRIP
ARTOO, IS THAT YOU?! OH THANK THE MAKER!
LOOK WHAT THEY'VE DONE TO ME!
WEE HOO BEEDA WIP
WHAT DO YOU MEAN, WHAT DID I NEED THEM FOR?! WHY, YOU CRUEL LITTLE...
WUUUYUU WRRRP WRRRP BUDDA
OH. OH, I SEE. OH MY.
MISTRESS LEIA...IF YOU CAN HEAR ME...CAPTAIN SOLO APPEARS TO BE IN RATHER SERIOUS DANGER.
BWOOP WOOBEEP THWWWK
YES, I'M TRYING TO CALL HER! HOLD STILL, YOU BLITHERING...

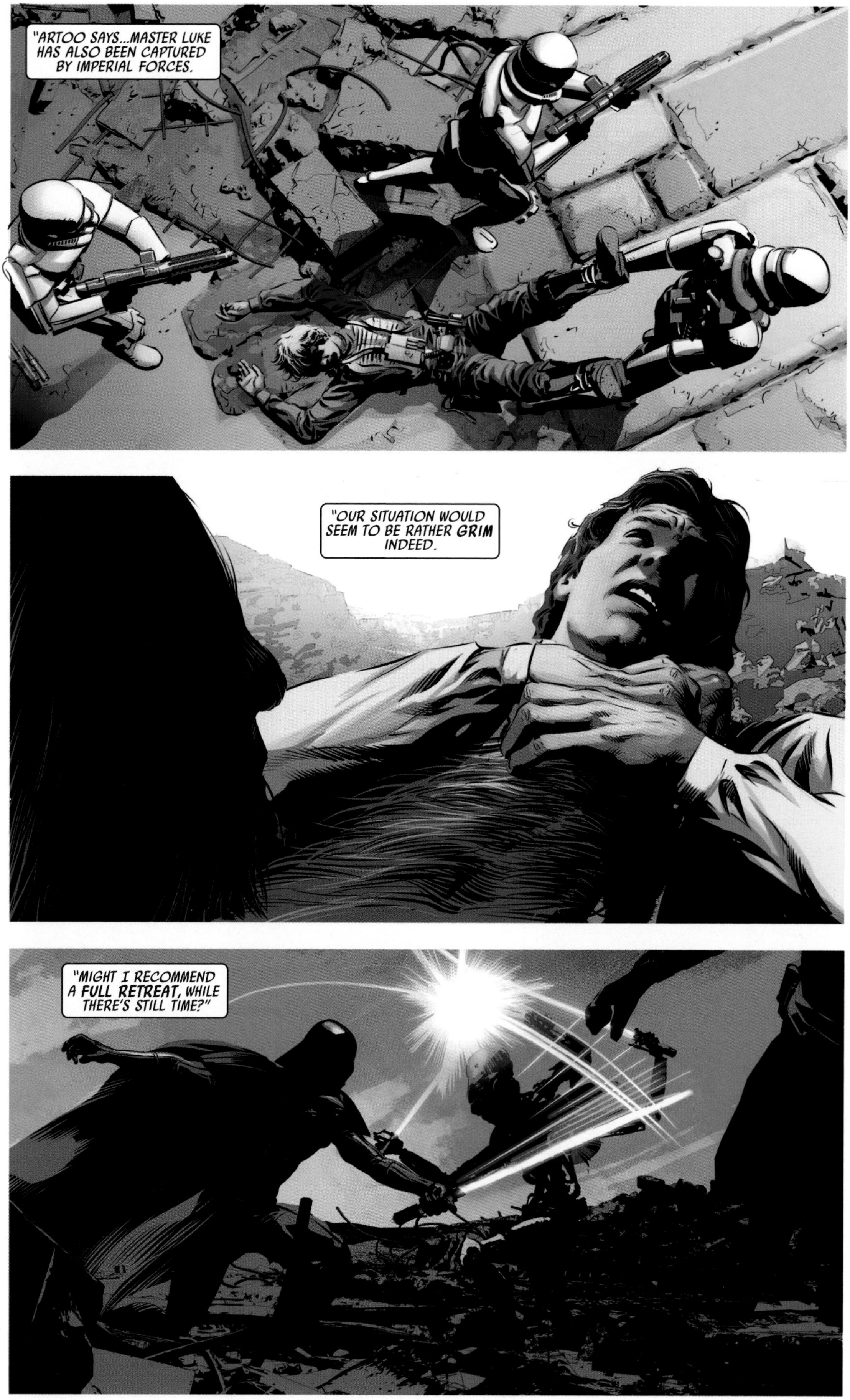
"ARTOO SAYS...MASTER LUKE HAS ALSO BEEN CAPTURED BY IMPERIAL FORCES.
"OUR SITUATION WOULD SEEM TO BE RATHER GRIM INDEED.
"MIGHT I RECOMMEND A FULL RETREAT, WHILE THERE'S STILL TIME?"

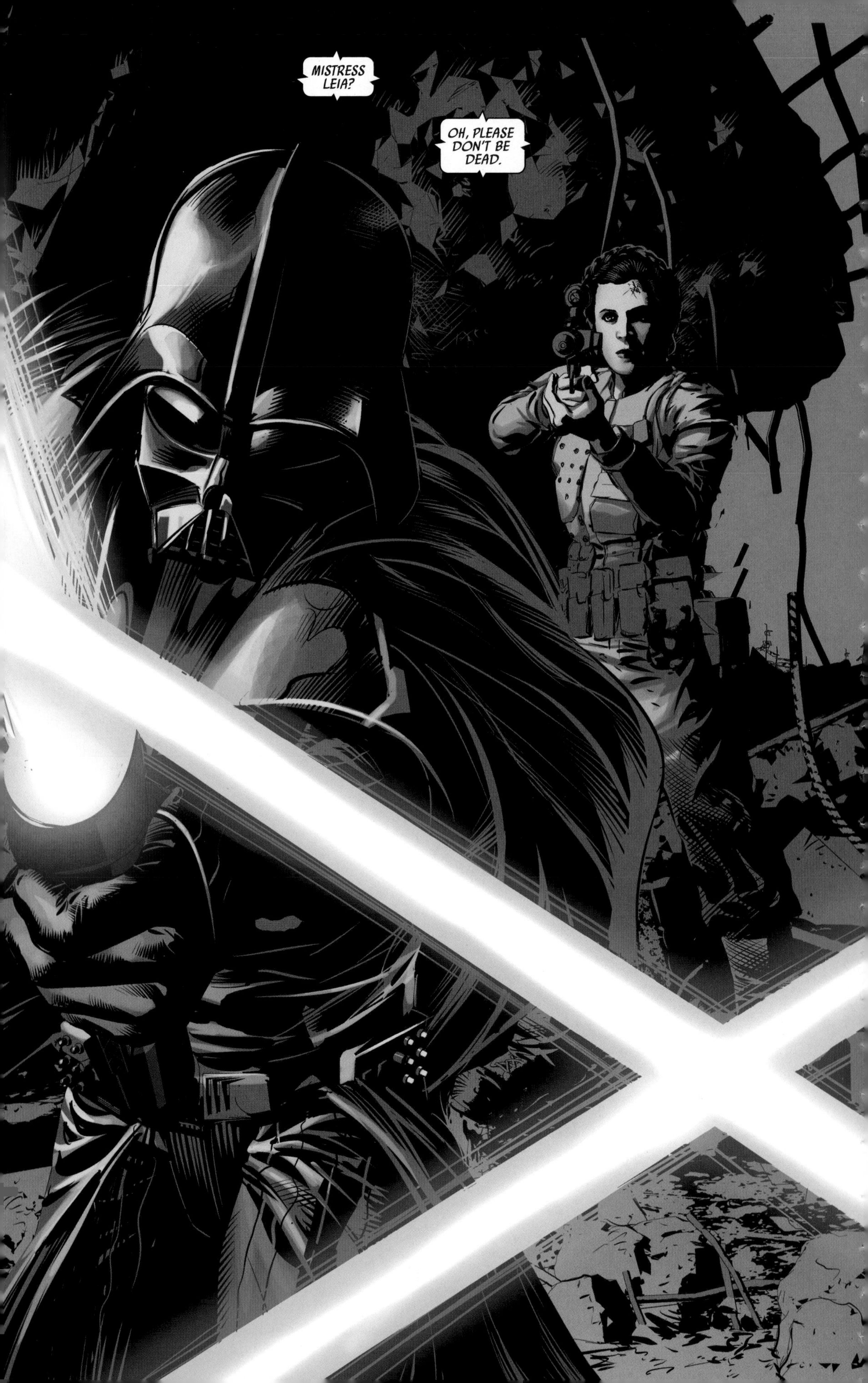
MISTRESS LEIA?
OH, PLEASE DON'T BE DEAD.

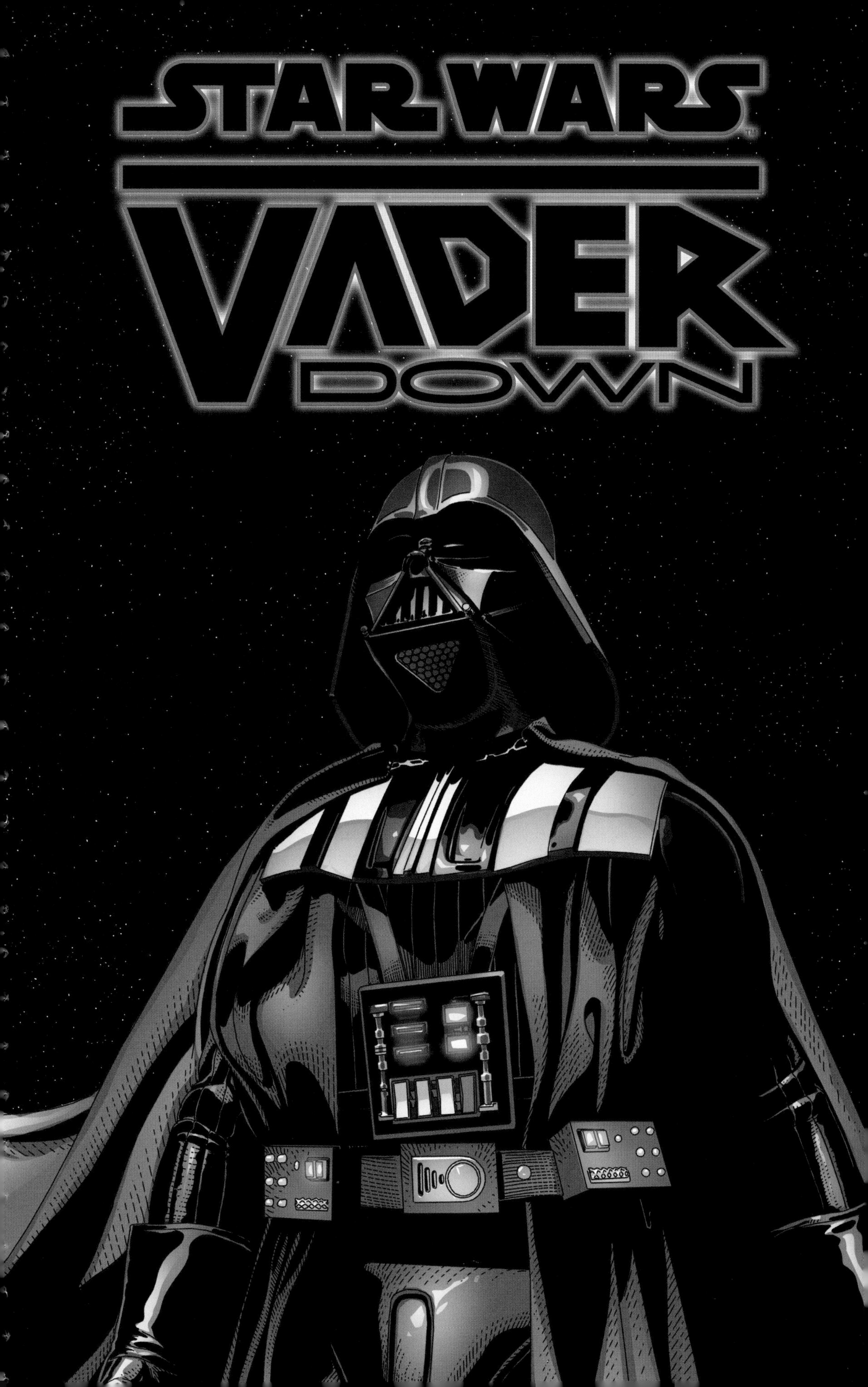
STAR WARS
VADER
DOWN

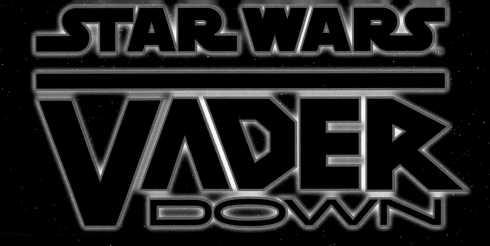

STAR WARS VADER DOWN

COLLECT THEM ALL!

Set of 6 Hardcover Books ISBN: 978-1-61479-560-5

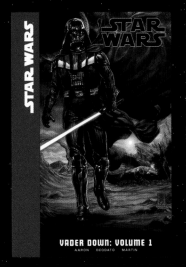

STAR WARS
STAR WARS
VADER DOWN: VOLUME 1
AARON DEODATO MARTIN

Hardcover Book ISBN
978-1-61479-561-2

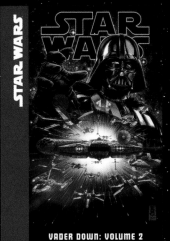

STAR WARS
STAR WARS
VADER DOWN: VOLUME 2
GILLEN LARROCA DELGADO

Hardcover Book ISBN
978-1-61479-562-9

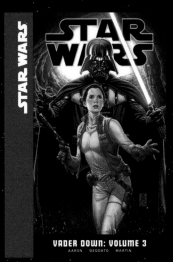

STAR WARS
STAR WARS
VADER DOWN: VOLUME 3
AARON DEODATO MARTIN

Hardcover Book ISBN
978-1-61479-563-6

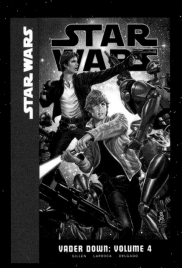

STAR WARS
STAR WARS
VADER DOWN: VOLUME 4
GILLEN LARROCA DELGADO

Hardcover Book ISBN
978-1-61479-564-3

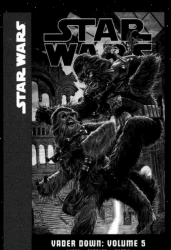

STAR WARS
STAR WARS
VADER DOWN: VOLUME 5
AARON DEODATO MARTIN

Hardcover Book ISBN
978-1-61479-565-0

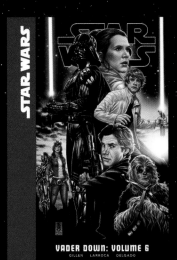

STAR WARS
STAR WARS
VADER DOWN: VOLUME 6
GILLEN LARROCA DELGADO

Hardcover Book ISBN
978-1-61479-566-7